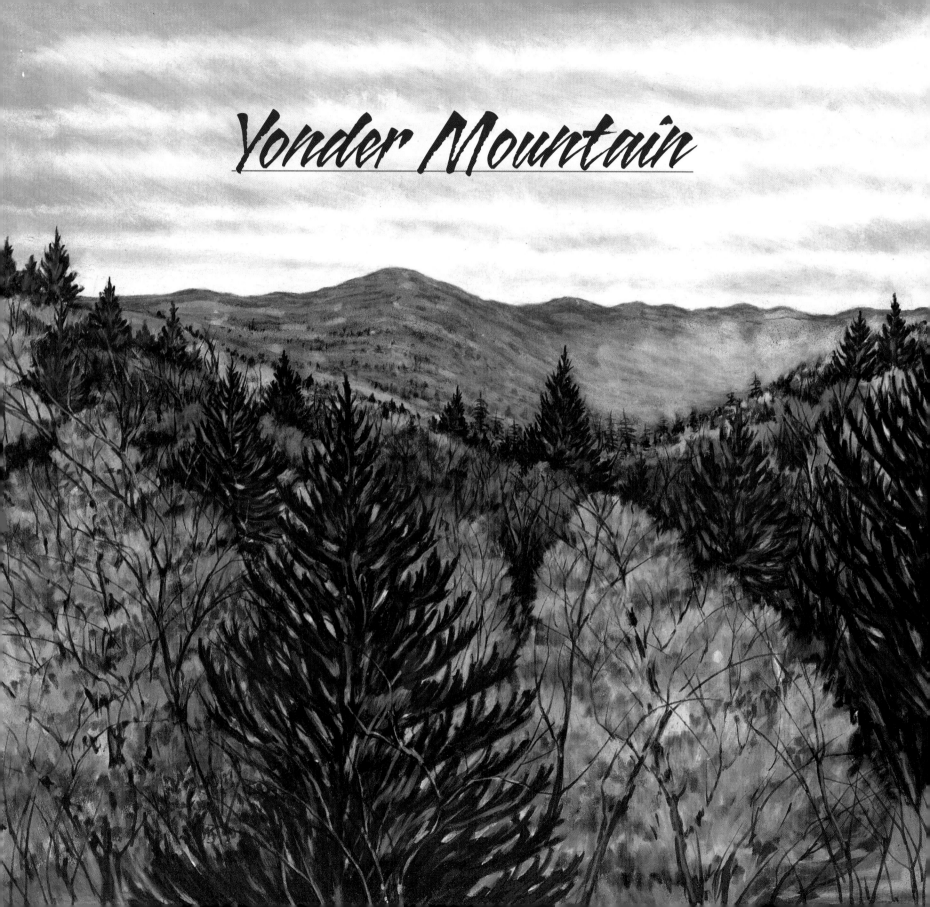

As told by Robert H. Bushyhead

Written by Kay Thorpe Bannon

Foreword by Joseph Bruchac

Illustrated by Kristina Rodanas

Yonder Mountain

A CHEROKEE LEGEND

MARSHALL CAVENDISH • NEW YORK

Library of Congress Cataloging-in-Publication Data
Bushyhead, Robert H.
Yonder mountain / as told by Robert H. Bushyhead ; written by Kay T. Bannon;
illustrated by Kristina Rodanas.   p.   cm.
Summary: A Cherokee chief chooses his successor by asking three candidates
to climb a mountain, thus testing their character and strength.
ISBN 0-7614-5113-7
1. Cherokee Indians—Folklore. 2. Legends—Southern States. [1. Cherokee Indians—Folklore.
2. Indians of North America—Southern States—Folklore. 3. Folklore—Southern States.]
I. Rodanas, Kristina, ill. II. Title.
E99.C5.B8887 2002   398.2'089'9755—dc21   [E]   2001032319

The text of this book is set in 14 point Galliard.
The illustrations are rendered in colored pencil and watercolor.
Printed in Malaysia
First edition
6 5 4 3 2 1

Dedicated to Mr. Bushyhead – K.T.B.

To Vanessa and Rex, with love – K.R.

Foreward

Few people have endured more than the people who are known popularly as the Cherokee, but call themselves Ani:yv:wiya—the Principal People. More than 1,400 of the Ani:yv:wiya managed to elude the terrible Trail of Tears and remain in a part of their former vast homeland at Qalla in the Smoky Mountains of western North Carolina. That area became the Eastern Cherokee Nation.

Most of the Cherokee folktales that have become popular, and even published as children's books, come from the North Carolina Cherokee and are drawn directly from the stories recorded in the late 1800s by ethnologist James Mooney in his classic 1900 volume *Myths of the Cherokees*. However, in contrast to these works, *Yonder Mountain* is not found in Mooney's book. It is a story told by a Cherokee elder who spent a lifetime in the service of his people. Passed down from one generation to the next in Reverend Robert H. Bushyhead's family, *Yonder Mountain* is a tale that is very much within Native tradition. How so? Is it because it was first told in the Kituhwa dialect of the Cherokee language, a language that Reverend Bushyhead has labored to restore to the children? In part. Is it because it comes

from the land that tradition says gave birth to the Principal People, land they have never left? That too, is part of the reason. But it should also be clear that this is a lesson story. In the old days, our children were not disciplined by physical punishment or by abuse of any kind. Instead, they were told stories which were so well-told that the children could not help but remember them . . . stories that were so full of teaching that they could not help but learn, even when they did not know they were learning. That was the tradition, a tradition truly honored by this tale.

Yonder Mountain is a wonderful teaching story. It is a great gift to the Ani: yw:wiya and to all those who have ears to hear and hearts that are open. I am so very glad to see this story in print and to know it will be shared for many more generations. And I say to Reverend Robert H. Bushyhead—as a young man who needs to learn might say to an elder—Wado Edudu, Wado. Thank you, Grandfather, thank you.

Joseph Bruchac

December 1998

Once in the land of the Cherokee people, there lived a beloved chief called Sky (kalv:lo:ʔi). Chief Sky had seen many summers and winters. He had led his people through long seasons of peace. He had seen their warriors go through great battles with enemies. But now his step was slow, and his hand trembled on the bow. He could no longer spot brother deer among the trees. He was no longer able to lead his people.

One day in the season of falling leaves, the chief called three young men (ani:wi:na) to him and said, "One of you will take my place and become chief and lead our people. But first, I must put you to the test."

Chief Sky turned slowly, looking into the distance. "Do you see yonder mountain?"

The three young men followed the gaze of their chief and saw a great mountain rising out of the mist in the distance. "Yes," they answered. "We see the mountain."

Chief Sky pointed toward the highest peak. "I want you to go to the mountaintop. Bring back to me what you find there."

The first young man called Black Bear (Yo:na) quickly started up the side of the mountain. After the sun reached the middle of the day, Black Bear came to a wide place in the trail where he stopped to rest. He leaned his head upon a rock, and his eyes grew heavy. Just as his eyes were closing, he caught sight of a thousand lights twinkling in the sun. Black Bear sat up straight and saw stones of great beauty lining each side of the trail. They sparkled and glowed in the sunlight. Black Bear examined a stone, carefully turning it over and over in his hand and watching the sun dance on each surface. "If my people had these stones, they would never be hungry again," he said. "We could trade them for food and our lives would be better."

Black Bear gathered many sparkling stones and ran down the mountain and back to his village. The people saw him coming and lined the path as he entered the village. The children pointed to the sparkling stones and said "See the pretty stones Black Bear has found." Black Bear handed the stones to Chief Sky and said, "My chief, look what I have found—beautiful stones! We can trade them for food and will never go hungry. We will be safe through many winters."

The chief smiled fondly upon the young man and said, "You have done well, my son. You have done well. Let us now wait for the others."

The second young man (awi:na) called Gray Wolf (Wah ya) climbed the mountain and went past the place of the sparkling stones. He climbed higher and higher. The trail became steep and rugged. Finally, he came to an open place where he rested beside the trail. As Gray Wolf leaned against a rock, he saw herbs, roots, and bark on each side of the trail. He picked an herb, looking closely at its pointed leaves and long roots. "These are the healing plants of our medicine man," he said. "If my people have these herbs and roots, they will no longer be sick and suffer. We could be healed with these plants." Gray Wolf gathered one of each of the plants and hurried down the mountain.

The people saw him coming and lined the pathway. The children waved and the elders said, "See all the herbs Gray Wolf has found. We will never be sick again!"

Gray Wolf ran to his chief and spread the plants before him. "Look, my Chief, what I have found. We no longer need to suffer. I have found all kinds of herbs, and we can be healed."

The old chief smiled fondly on Gray Wolf and said, "You have done well, my son. You have done well. Now let us wait for Soaring Eagle (Uwoh?li), our last young man.

They waited. Days went by and Soaring Eagle did not return. Still the village waited. After six days, the people began to murmur. "Something must have happened to Soaring Eagle. Why wait any longer?" But Chief Sky said to his people, "We will wait one day longer." And so they waited.

On the seventh day, as the sun cast its long shadow over the village, the people saw Soaring Eagle coming. He stumbled with bleeding feet. His clothes were ripped and torn. He held nothing in his hands.

The people were quiet as Soaring Eagle fell at the feet of his chief. Soaring Eagle spoke softly to Chief Sky. "I went to the top of the mountain, my chief. But I bring back nothing in my hands. I passed a place where there were sparkling stones, but I remembered you said go to the top of the mountain. I passed a place where all sorts of herbs grew, but I remembered your words. The path was rough. There were great cliffs and sharp rocks. I have nothing in my hands to show you, but I bring back a story from the top of the mountain."

The old chief put his hand on the shoulder of the young man. "Tell us your story, my son."

Soaring Eagle began. "As I stood on yonder mountain and looked across the valley and beyond the farthest mountain, I saw a smoke signal. It was a signal calling for help. The signal said 'We are dying,' and then 'Come and help us.'"

Soaring Eagle rose to his feet. "Chief Sky," he pleaded. "We need to go to them quickly. They are in trouble."

Chief Sky stood straight before his people and the three young men. Pausing for a time, he lifted his eyes to the mountains and watched the mist settle on the peaks. He then turned to his people and spoke. "We need a leader who has climbed to the top of the mountain. We need one who has seen beyond the mountain to other people who are in need."

The people watched as Chief Sky carefully began to remove his robe. He turned to face Soaring Eagle. "You, my son, shall wear the chief's robe," the beloved old leader declared. Chief Sky placed the robe over the torn clothing of the chosen young man. "You shall be our next chief, Soaring Eagle. You will lead our people and help those in need. Yes, you will be our chief and help us climb yonder mountain."

Glossary

Below are a few English words with the Cherokee translation. The translations have been specially written using the English alphabet so that you can sound them out.

Bear	Yo:na	Wolf	Wah ya
Eagle	Uwohaʔli	young man	awi:na
Sky	Kalv:lo:ʔI	young men	ani:wi:na